Helen Gray Cone

The ride to the lady

And other poems

Helen Gray Cone

The ride to the lady
And other poems

ISBN/EAN: 9783743328297

Manufactured in Europe, USA, Canada, Australia, Japa

Cover: Foto ©Andreas Hilbeck / pixelio.de

Manufactured and distributed by brebook publishing software
(www.brebook.com)

Helen Gray Cone

The ride to the lady

THE RIDE TO THE LADY

And Other Poems

BY

HELEN GRAY CONE

BOSTON AND NEW YORK
HOUGHTON, MIFFLIN AND COMPANY
The Riverside Press, Cambridge
1893

The Riverside Press, Cambridge, Mass., U. S. A.
Electrotyped and Printed by H. O. Houghton & Co.

CONTENTS

		PAGE
The Ride to the Lady	. . . .	5
The First Guest	. . . .	9
Silence	. . . .	12
Arraignment	. . . .	14
The Going Out of the Tide	. . . .	16
King Raedwald	. . . .	19
Ivo of Chartres	. . . .	23
Madonna Pia	. . . .	26
Two Moods of Failure	. . . .	31
The Story of the " Orient "	. . . .	37
A Resurrection	. . . .	42
The Glorious Company	. . . .	44
The Trumpeter	. . . .	46
Comrades	. . . .	48
The House of Hate	. . . .	50
The Arrowmaker	. . . .	53
A Nest in a Lyre	. . . .	56
Thisbe	. . . .	57
The Spring Beauties	. . . .	58
Kinship	. . . .	60
Compensation	. . . .	62
When Willows Green	. . . .	63
At the Parting of the Ways	. . . .	64

The Fair Gray Lady 67

The Encounter 68

Summer Hours 72

Love Unsung 73

The Wish for a Chaplet 74

Sonnets :

    The Torch Race 77

    To Sleep 78

    Sister Snow 79

    Retrospect 80

    The Contrast 81

    A Mystery 82

    Triumph 84

    In Winter, with the Book we read in Spring . . . 85

    Sere Wisdom 87

    Isolation 89

    The Lost Dryad 90

    A Memory 91

    The Gifts of the Oak 92

    The Strayed Singer 94

    The Immortal Word 95

THE RIDE TO THE LADY

"Now since mine even is come at last, —
For I have been the sport of steel,
And hot life ebbeth from me fast,
And I in saddle roll and reel, —
Come bind me, bind me on my steed !
Of fingering leech I have no need ! "
The chaplain clasped his mailèd knee.
"Nor need I more thy whine and thee !
No time is left my sins to tell ;
But look ye bind me, bind me well ! "
They bound him strong with leathern thong,
For the ride to the lady should be long.

Day was dying ; the poplars fled,
Thin as ghosts, on a sky blood-red ;
Out of the sky the fierce hue fell,
And made the streams as the streams of hell.
All his thoughts as a river flowed,
Flowed aflame as fleet he rode,

Onward flowed to her abode,
Ceased at her feet, mirrored her face.
(Viewless Death apace, apace,
Rode behind him in that race.)

" Face, mine own, mine alone,
Trembling lips my lips have known,
Birdlike stir of the dove-soft eyne
Under the kisses that make them mine!
Only of thee, of thee, my need!
Only to thee, to thee, I speed!"
The Cross flashed by at the highway's turn;
In a beam of the moon the Face shone stern.

Far behind had the fight's din died;
The shuddering stars in the welkin wide
Crowded, crowded, to see him ride.
The beating hearts of the stars aloof
Kept time to the beat of the horse's hoof.
"What is the throb that thrills so sweet?
Heart of my lady, I feel it beat!"
But his own strong pulse the fainter fell,
Like the failing tongue of a hushing bell.
The flank of the great-limbed steed was wet
Not alone with the started sweat.

Fast, and fast, and the thick black wood
Arched its cowl like a black friar's hood ;
Fast, and fast, and they plunged therein, —
But the viewless rider rode to win.

Out of the wood to the highway's light
Galloped the great-limbed steed in fright ;
The mail clashed cold, and the sad owl cried,
And the weight of the dead oppressed his side.

Fast, and fast, by the road he knew ;
And slow, and slow, the stars withdrew ;
And the waiting heaven turned weirdly blue,
As a garment worn of a wizard grim.
He neighed at the gate in the morning dim.

She heard no sound before her gate,
Though very quiet was her bower.
All was as her hand had left it late :
The needle slept on the broidered vine,
Where the hammer and spikes of the passion-
        flower
Her fashioning did wait.
On the couch lay something fair,
With steadfast lips and veilèd eyne ;

But the lady was not there.
On the wings of shrift and prayer,
Pure as winds that winnow snow,
Her soul had risen twelve hours ago.
The burdened steed at the barred gate stood,
No whit the nearer to his goal.
Now God's great grace assoil the soul
That went out in the wood !

THE FIRST GUEST

When the house is finished, Death enters.

Eastern Proverb.

LIFE's House being ready all,
Each chamber fair and dumb,
Ere Life, the Lord, is come
With pomp into his hall, —
Ere Toil has trod the floors,
Ere Love has lit the fires,
Or young great-eyed Desires
Have, timid, tried the doors ;
Or from east-window leaned
One Hope, to greet the sun,
Or one gray Sorrow screened
Her sight against the west, —
Then enters the first guest,
The House of Life being done.

He waits there in the shade.
I deem he is Life's twin,
For whom the House was made.

9

Whatever his true name,
Be sure, to enter in
He has both key and claim.

The daybeams, free of fear,
Creep drowsy toward his feet;
His heart were heard to beat,
Were any there to hear;
Ah, not for ends malign,
Like wild thing crouched in lair,
Or watcher of a snare,
But with a friend's design
He lurks in shadow there!

He goes not to the gates
To welcome any other,
Nay, not Lord Life, his brother;
But still his hour awaits
Each several guest to find
Alone, yea, quite alone;
Pacing with pensive mind
The cloister's echoing stone,
Or singing, unaware,
At the turning of the stair.
'T is truth, though we forget,

In Life's House enters none
Who shall that seeker shun,
Who shall not so be met.
" Is this mine hour ? " each saith.
" So be it, gentle Death ! "
Each has his way to end,
Encountering this friend.
Griefs die to memories mild ;
Hope turns a weanèd child ;
Love shines a spirit white,
With eyes of deepened light.
When many a guest has passed,
Some day 't is Life's at last
To front the face of Death.
Then, casements closed, men say :
" Lord Life is gone away ;
He went, we trust and pray,
To God, who gave him breath."
Beginning, End, He is :
Are not these sons both His ?
Lo, these with Him are one !
To phrase it so were best :
God's self is that first Guest,
The House of Life being done !

SILENCE

WHY should I sing of earth or heaven? not
    rather rest,
Powerless to speak of that which hath my soul
    possessed, —
For full possession dumb?   Yea, Silence,
    that were best.

And though for what it failed to sound I brake
    the string,
And dashed the sweet lute down, a too-much-
    fingered thing,
And found a wild new voice, — oh, still, why
    should I sing?

An earth-song could I make, strange as the
    breath of earth,
Filled with the great calm joy of life and death
    and birth?
Yet, were it less than this, the song were little
    worth.

For this the fields express ; brown clods tell
    each to each ;
Sad-colored leaves have sense whereto I can-
    not reach ;
Spiced everlasting-flowers outstrip my range of
    speech.

A heaven-song could I make, all fire that yet
    was peace,
And tenderness not lost, though glory did in-
    crease ?
But were it less than this, 't were well the song
    should cease.

For this the still west saith, with plumy flames
    bestrewn ;
Heaven's body sapphire-clear, at stirless height
    of noon ;
The cloud where lightnings pulse, beside the
    untroubled moon.

I will not sing of earth or heaven, but rather rest,
Rapt by the face of heaven, and held on earth's
    warm breast.
Hushed lips, a beating heart, yea, Silence, that
    were best.

ARRAIGNMENT

"Not ye who have stoned, not ye who have
   smitten us," cry
   The sad, great souls, as they go out hence
      into dark,
   "Not ye we accuse, though for you was our
      passion borne ;
And ye we reproach not, who silently passed
      us by.
   We forgive blind eyes and the ears that
      would not hark,
   The careless and causeless hate and the
      shallow scorn.

"But ye, who have seemed to know us, have
      seen and heard ;
   Who have set us at feasts and have crowned
      with the costly rose ;
   Who have spread us the purple of praises
      beneath our feet ;

Yet guessed not the word that we spake was a
    living word,
Applauding the sound, — we account you as
    worse than foes !
We sobbed you our message ; ye 'said, ' It is
    song, and sweet ! ' "

THE GOING OUT OF THE TIDE

THE eastern heaven was all faint amethyst,
Whereon the moon hung dreaming in the mist;
To north yet drifted one long delicate plume
Of roseate cloud; like snow the ocean-spume.

Now when the first foreboding swiftly ran
Through the loud-glorying sea that it began
To lose its late-gained lordship of the land,
Uprose the billow like an angered man,
And flung its prone strength far along the sand;
Almost, almost to the old bound, the dark
And taunting triumph-mark.

But no, no, no! and slow, and slow, and slow,
Like a heart losing hold, this wave must go, —
Must go, must go, — dragged heavily back,
      back,
Beneath the next wave plunging on its track,
Charging, with thunderous and defiant shout,
To fore-determined rout.

Again, again the unexhausted main
Renews fierce effort, drawing force unguessed
From awful deeps of its mysterious breast :
Like arms of passionate protest, tossed in vain,
The spray upflings above the billow's crest.
Again the appulse, again the backward
　　strain —
Till ocean must have rest.

With one abandoned movement, swift and
　　wild, —
As though bowed head and outstretched arms
　　it laid
On the earth's lap, soft-sobbing, — hushed and
　　stayed,
The great sea quiets, like a soothèd child.
Ha ! what sharp memory clove the calm, and
　　drave
This last fleet furious wave ?

On, on, endures the struggle into night,
Ancient as Time, yet fresh as the fresh hour ;
As oft repeated since the birth of light
As the strong agony and mortal fight
Of human souls, blind-reaching, with the
　　Power

Aloof, unmoved, impossible to cross,
Whose law is seeming loss.

Low-sunken from the longed-for triumph-mark,
The spent sea sighs as one that grieves in sleep.
The unveiled moon along the rippling plain
Casts many a keen, cold, shifting silvery spark,
Wild as the pulses of strange joy, that leap
Even in the quick of pain.

And she compelling, she that stands for law, —
As law for Will eternal, — perfect, clear,
And uncompassionate shines : to her appear
Vast sequences close-linked without a flaw.
All past despairs of ocean unforgot,
All raptures past, serene her light she gives,
The moon too high for pity, since she lives
Aware that loss is not.

KING RAEDWALD

WILL you hear now the speech of King Raed-
    wald, — heathen Raedwald, the simple
    yet wise ?
He, the ruler of North-folk and South-folk, a
    man open-browed as the skies,
Held the eyes of the eager Italians with his
    blue, bold, Englishman's eyes.

In his hall, on his throne, so he sat, with the
    light of the fire on him full :
Colored bright as the ring of red gold on his
    hand, fit to buffet a bull,
Was the mane that grew down on his neck, was
    the beard he would pondering pull.

To the priests, to the eager Italians, thus fear-
    less he poured his free speech :
"O my honey-tongued fathers, I turn not away
    from the faith that ye teach !

Not the less hath a man many moods, and
    may ask a religion for each.

"Grant that all things are well with the realm
    on a delicate day of the spring,
Easter month, time of hopes and of swallows !
    The praises, the psalms that ye sing,
As in pleasant accord they float heavenward,
    are good in the ears of the king.

" Then the heart bubbles forth with clear wa-
    ters, to the tune of this wonder-word
    Peace,
From the chanting and preaching whereof ye
    who serve the white Christ never cease ;
And your curly, soft incense ascending enwraps
    my content like a fleece.

" But a churl comes adrip from the rivers,
    pants me out, fallen spent on the floor,
'O King Raedwald, Northumberland marches,
    and to-morrow knocks hard at thy door,
Hot for melting thy crown on the hearth !'
    Then commend me to Woden and Thor !

" Could I sit then and listen to preachments
    on turning the cheek to the blow,
And saying a prayer for the smiter, and holding
    my seen treasure low
For the sake of a treasure unseen ? By the
    sledge of the Thunderer, no!

" For my thought flashes out as a sword, cleav-
    ing counsel as clottage of cream ;
And your incense and chanting are but as the
    smoke of burnt towns and the scream ;
And I quaff me the thick mead of triumph
    from enemies' skulls in my dream !

" And 't is therefore this day I resolve me, —
    for King Raedwald will cringe not, nor
    lie ! —
I will bring back the altar of Woden ; in the
    temple will have it, hard by
The new altar of this your white Christ. As
    my mood may decide, worship I ! "

So he spake in his large self-reliance, — he, a
    man open-browed as the skies ;
Would not measure his soul by a standard that
    was womanish-weak to his eyes,

Smite his breast and go on with his sinning,
  — savage Raedwald, the simple yet
  wise !

And the centuries bloom o'er his barrow.   But
  for us, — have we mastered it quite,
The old riddle, that sweet is strong's outcome,
  the old marvel, that meekness is might,
That the child is the leader of lions, that for-
  giveness is force at its height ?

When we summon the shade of rude Raedwald,
  in his candor how king-like he towers !
Have the centuries, over his slumber, only
  borne sterile falsehoods for flowers ?
Pray you, what if Christ found him the nobler,
  having weighed his frank manhood with
  ours ?

IVO OF CHARTRES

Now may it please my lord, Louis the king,
  Lily of Christ and France! riding his quest,
I, Bishop Ivo, saw a wondrous thing.

  There was no light of sun left in the west,
And slowly did the moon's new light increase.
  Heaven, without cloud, above the near hill's
     crest,
Lay passion-purple in a breathless peace.
  Stars started like still tears, in rapture shed,
Which without consciousness the lids release.

  All steadily, one little sparkle red,
Afar, drew close. A woman's form grew up
  Out of the dimness, tall, with queen-like head,
And in one hand was fire; in one, a cup.
  Of aspect grave she was, with eyes upraised,
As one whose thoughts perpetually did sup
  At the Lord's table.

While the cresset blazed,
Her I regarded. "Daughter, whither bent,
  And wherefore ? " As by speech of man
    amazed,
One moment her deep look to me she lent ;
  Then, in a voice of hymn-like, solemn fall,
Calm, as by rote, she spake out her intent :

"I in my cruse bear water, wherewithal
To quench the flames of Hell ; and with my
    fire
  I Paradise would burn : that hence no small
Fear shall impel, and no mean hope shall hire,
  Men to serve God as they have served of
    yore ;
But to his will shall set their whole desire,
  For love, love, love alone, forevermore ! "

And ." love, love, love," rang round her as she
    passed
  From sight, with mystic murmurs o'er and
    o'er
Reverbed from hollow heaven, as from some
    vast,
  Deep-colored, vaulted, ocean-answering shell.

I, Ivo, had no power to ban or bless,
But was as one withholden by a spell.
Forward she fared in lofty loneliness,
Urged on by an imperious inward stress,
To waste fair Eden, and to drown fierce Hell.

MADONNA PIA

Ricordati di me, che son la Pia.
Siena mi fe ; disfecemi Maremma :
Salsi colui, che, inanellata pria,
Disposato m' avea colla sua gemma.

Purgatorio, Canto V.

To westward lies the unseen sea,
  Blue sea the live winds wander o'er.
The many-colored sails can flee,
  And leave the dead, low-lying shore.
Her longing does not seek the main,
  Her face turns northward first at morn ;
There, crowning all the wide champaign,
  Siena stood, where she was born.

Siena stands, and still shall stand ;
  She ne'er shall see or town or tower.
Warm life and beauty, hand in hand,
  Steal farther from her hour by hour.
Yet forth she leans, with trembling knees,
  And northward will she stare and stare

Through that thick wall of cypress-trees,
  And sigh adown the stirless air :

" Shall no remembrance in Siena linger
  Of me, once fair, whom slow Maremma
    slays ?
As well he knows, whose ring upon my finger
  Hath sealed for his alone. mine earthly
    days ! "

From wilds where shudders through the weeds
  The dull, mean-headed, silent snake,
Like voiceless doubt that creeps and breeds ;
  From swamps where sluggish waters take,
As lives unblest a passing love,
  The flag-flower's image in the spring,
Or seem, when flits the bird above,
  To stir within with shadowed wing,

A Presence mounts in pallid mist
  To fold her close : she breathes its breath ;
She waxes wan, by Fever kissed,
  Who weds her for his master, Death.
Aside are set her dimmed hopes all,
  She counts no more the uncurrent hoard ;

On gray Death's neck she fain would fall,
    To own him for her proper lord.

She minds the journey here by night:
    When some red sudden torch would blaze,
She saw by fits, with childish fright,
    The cork-trees twist beside the ways.
Like dancing demon shapes they showed,
    With malice drunk; the bat beat by,
The owlet sobbed; on, on they rode,
    She knew not where, she knows not why.

For Nello, — when in piteous wise
    She lifted up her look to ask,
Except the ever-burning eyes
    His face was like a marble mask.
And so it always meets her now;
    The tomb wherein at last he lies
Shall bear such carven lips and brow,
    All save the ever-burning eyes.

Perchance it is his form alone
    Doth stroke his hound, at meat doth sit,
And, for the soul that was his own,
    A fiend awhile inhabits it;

While he sinks through the fiery throng,
 Down, down, to fill an evil bond,
Since false conceit of others' wrong
 Hath wrought him to a sin beyond.

But she, — if when her years were glad
 Vain fluttering thoughts were hers, that hid
Behind that gracious fame she had ;
 If e'er observance hard she did
That sinful men might call her saint, —
 White-handed Pia, dovelike-eyed, —
The sick blank hours shall yet acquaint
 Her heart with all her blameful pride.

And Death shall find her kneeling low,
 And lift her to the porphyry stair,
And she from ledge to ledge shall go,
 Stayed by the staff of that last prayer,
Until the high, sweet-singing wood
 Whence folk are rapt to heaven, she win ;
Therein the unpardoned never stood,
 Nor may one Sorrow nest therein.

But through the Tuscan land shall beat
 Her Sorrow, like a wounded bird ;

And if her suit at Mary's feet
   Avail, its moan shall yet be heard
By some just poet, who shall shed,
   Whate'er the theme that leads his rhyme,
Bright words like tears above her, dead,
   Entreating of the after-time :

" Among you let her mournful memory linger !
   Siena bare her, whom Maremma slew ;
And that dark lord, who gave her maiden
     finger
   His ancient gem, the secret only knew."

TWO MOODS OF FAILURE

I

THE LAST CUP OF CANARY

SIR HARRY LOVELOCK, 1645

So, the powder 's low, and the larder 's clean,
  And surrender drapes, with its blacks im-
    pending,
All the stage for a sorry and sullen scene :
  Yet indulge me my whim of a madcap end-
    ing !

Let us once more fill, ere the final chill,
  Every vein with the glow of the rich canary !
Since the sweet hot liquor of life's to spill,
  Of the last of the cellar what boots be chary ?

Then hear the conclusion : I 'll yield my breath,
  But my leal old house and my good blade
    never !

Better one bitter kiss on the lips of Death
  Than despoiled Defeat as a wife forever !

Let the faithful fire hold the walls in ward
  Till the roof-tree crash ! Be the smoke once
    riven
While we flash from the gate like a single
    sword,
  True steel to the hilt, though in dull earth
    driven !

Do you frown, Sir Richard, above your ruff,
  In the Holbein yonder ? My deed ensures
    you !
For the flame like a fencer shall give rebuff
  To your blades that blunder, you Round-
    head boors, you !

And my ladies, a-row on the gallery wall,
  Not a sing-song sergeant or corporal sainted
Shall pierce their breasts with his Puritan ball,
  To annul the charms of the flesh, though
    painted !

I have worn like a jewel the life they gave ;
  As the ring in mine ear I can lightly lose it.

If my days be done, why, my days were
 brave !
If the end arrive, I as master choose it !

Then fill to the brim, and a health, I say,
 To our liege King Charles, and I pray God
 bless him !
'T would amend worse vintage to drink dismay
 To the clamorous mongrel pack that press
 him !

And a health to the fair women, past recall,
 That like birds astray through the heart's
 hall flitted ;
To the lean devil Failure last of all,
 And the lees in his beard for a fiend out-
 witted !

II

THE YOUNG MAN CHARLES STUART REVIEW-
ETH THE TROOPS ON BLACKHEATH

(PRIVATE CONSTANT-IN-TRIBULATION JOYCE, *May*, 1660)

WE were still as a wood without wind ; as
 't were set by a spell

Stayed the gleam on the steel-cap, the glint on
the slant petronel.
He to left of me drew down his grim grizzled
lip with his teeth, —
I remember his look; so we grew like dumb
trees on the heath.

But the people, — the people were mad as
with store of new wine;
Oh, they cheered him, they capped him, they
roared as he rode down the line:
He that fled us at Worcester, the boy, the green
brier-shoot, the son
Of the Stuart on whom for his sin the great
judgment was done!

Swam before us the field of our shame, and
our souls walked afar;
Saw the glory, the blaze of the sun bursting
over Dunbar;
Saw the faces of friends, in the morn riding
jocund to fight;
Saw the stern pallid faces again, as we saw
them at night!

"O ye blessed, who died in the Lord! would
    to God that we too
Had so passed, only sad that we ceased his
    high justice to do,
With the words of the psalm on our lips that
    from Israel's once came,
How the Lord is a strong man of war; yea,
    the Lord is his name!

"Not for us, not for us! who have served for
    his kingdom seven years,
Yea, and yet other seven have we served,
    sweating blood, bleeding tears,
For the kingdom of God and the saints!
    Rachel's beauty made bold,
Yet we bear but a Leah at last to a hearth
    that is cold!"

Burned the fire while I mused, while I gloomed;
    in the end came a call;
Settled o'er me a calm like a cloud, spake a
    voice still and small:
"Take thou Leah to bride, take thou Failure
    to bed and to board!
Thou shalt rear up new strengths at her knees;
    she is given of the Lord!

" If with weight of his right hand, with power,
    he denieth to deal,
And the smoke-clouds, and thunders of guns,
    and the lightnings of steel,
Shall the cool silent dews of his grace, in a
    season of peace,
Not descend on the land, as of old, for a sign,
    on the fleece?

" Hath he cleft not the rock, to the yield of a
    stream that is sweet?
Hath he set in the ribs of the lion no honey for
    meat?
Can he bring not delight to the desert, and
    buds to the rod?
He will shine, he will visit his vine; he hath
    sworn, he is God! "

Then I thought of the gate I rode through on
    the roan that 's long dead, —
I remember the dawn was but pale, and the
    stars overhead;
Of the babe that is grown to a maid, and of
    Martha, my wife,
And the spring on the wolds far away, and
    gave thanks for my life!

THE STORY OF THE "ORIENT"

'T was a pleasant Sunday morning while the
    spring was in its glory,
English spring of gentle glory; smoking by his
    cottage door,
Florid-faced, the man-o'-war's-man told his
    white-head boy the story,
Noble story of Aboukir, told a hundred times
    before.

" Here, the *Theseus* — here, the *Vanguard;* " as
    he spoke each name sonorous, —
Minotaur, Defence, Majestic, stanch old com-
    rades of the brine,
That against the ships of Brueys made their
    broadsides roar in chorus, —
Ranging daisies on his doorstone, deft he
    mapped the battle-line.

Mapped the curve of tall three-deckers, deft as
    might a man left-handed,

Who had given an arm to England later on at
    Trafalgar.
While he poured the praise of Nelson to the
    child with eyes expanded,
Bright athwart his honest forehead blushed the
    scarlet cutlass-scar.

For he served aboard the *Vanguard*, saw the
    Admiral blind and bleeding
Borne below by silent sailors, borne to die as
    then they deemed.
Every stout heart sick but stubborn, fought the
    sea-dogs on unheeding,
Guns were cleared and manned and cleared,
    the   battle   thundered,   flashed,   and
    screamed.

Till a cry swelled loud and louder, — towered
    on fire the *Orient* stately,
Brueys' flag-ship, she that carried guns a hun-
    dred and a score ;
Then came groping up the hatchway he they
    counted dead but lately,
Came the little one-armed Admiral to guide the
    fight once more.

" ' Lower the boats ! ' was Nelson's order." —
    But the listening boy beside him,
Who had followed all his motions with an
    eager wide blue eye,
Nursed upon the name of Nelson till he half
    had deified him,
Here, with childhood's crude consistence, broke
    the tale to question " Why ? "

For by children facts go streaming in a throng
    that never pauses,
Noted not, till, of a sudden, thought, a sun-
    beam, gilds the motes.
All at once the known words quicken, and the
    child would deal with causes.
Since to kill the French was righteous, why
    bade Nelson lower the boats ?

Quick the man put by the question. " But the
    Orient, none could save her ;
We could see the ships, the ensigns, clear as
    daylight by the flare ;
And a many leaped and left her ; but, God
    rest 'em ! some were braver ;
Some held by her, firing steady till she blew to
    God knows where."

At the shock, he said, the *Vanguard* shook
    through all her timbers oaken ;
It was like the shock of Doomsday, — not a
    tar but shuddered hard.
All was hushed for one strange moment ; then
    that awful calm was broken
By the heavy plash that answered the descent
    of mast and yard.

So, her cannon still defying, and her colors
    flaming, flying,
In her pit her wounded helpless, on her deck
    her Admiral dead,
Soared the *Orient* into darkness with her living
    and her dying :
" Yet our lads made shift to rescue three-score
    souls," the seaman said.

Long the boy with knit brows wondered o'er
    that friending of the foeman ;
Long the man with shut lips pondered ; power-
    less he to tell the cause
Why the brother in his bosom that desired the
    death of no man,
In the crash of battle wakened, snapped the
    bonds of hate like straws.

While he mused, his toddling maiden drew the
    daisies to a posy ;
Mild the bells of Sunday morning rang across
    the church-yard sod ;
And, helped on by tender hands, with sturdy
    feet all bare and rosy,
Climbed his babe to mother's breast, as climbs
    the slow world up to God.

A RESURRECTION

Neither would they be persuaded, though one rose from the dead.

I WAS quick in the flesh, was warm, and the
    live heart shook my breast ;
  In the market I bought and sold, in the tem-
    ple I bowed my head.
I had swathed me in shows and forms, and was
    honored above the rest
  For the sake of the life I lived ; nor did any
    esteem me dead.

But at last, when the hour was ripe — was it
    sudden-remembered word ?
  Was it sight of a bird that mounted, or sound
    of a strain that stole ?
I was 'ware of a spell that snapped, of an in-
    ward strength that stirred,
  Of a Presence that filled that place ; and it
    shone, and I knew my Soul.

And the dream I had called my life was a
    garment about my feet,
  For the web of the years was rent with the
    throe of a yearning strong.
With a sweep as of winds in heaven, with a
    rush as of flames that meet,
  The Flesh and the Spirit clasped; and I
    cried, "Was I dead so long?"

I had glimpse of the Secret, flashed through
    the symbol obscure and mean,
  And I felt as a fire what erst I repeated with
    lips of clay;
And I knew for the things eternal the things
    eye hath not seen;
  Yea, the heavens and the earth shall pass;
    but they never shall pass away.

And the miracle on me wrought, in the streets
    I would straight make known:
  "When this marvel of mine is heard, with-
    out cavil shall men receive
Any legend of haloed saint, starting up through
    the sealèd stone!"
  So I spake in the trodden ways; but behold,
    there would none believe!

" FACES, faces, faces of the streaming marching
    surge,
    Streaming on the weary road, toward the aw-
        ful steep,
Whence your glow and glory, as ye set to that
    sharp verge,
    Faces lit as sunlit stars, shining as ye sweep?

" Whence this wondrous radiance that ye some-
        how catch and cast,
    Faces rapt, that one discerns 'mid the dusky
        press
Herding in dull wonder, gathering fearful to
    the Vast?
    Surely all is dark before, night of nothing-
        ness ! "

Lo, the Light! (they answer) *O the pure, the
pulsing Light,*

Beating like a heart of life, like a heart of love,
Soaring, searching, filling all the breadth and
depth and height,
Welling, whelming with its peace worlds below,
above !

"O my soul, how art thou to that living
  Splendor blind,
 Sick with thy desire to see even as these
  men see ! —
Yet to look upon them is to know that God
  hath shined :
 Faces lit as sunlit stars, be all my light to
  me ! "

THE TRUMPETER

Two ships, alone in sky and sea,
  Hang clinched, with crash and roar;
There is but one — whiche'er it be —
  Will ever come to shore.

And will it be the grim black bulk,
  That towers so evil now?
Or will it be The Grace of God,
  With the angel at her prow?

The man that breathes the battle's breath
  May live at last to know;
But the trumpeter lies sick to death
  In the stifling dark below.

He hears the fight above him rave;
  He fears his mates must yield;
He lies as in a narrow grave
  Beneath a battle-field.

His fate will fall before the ship's,
    Whate'er the ship betide ;
He lifts the trumpet to his lips
    As though he kissed a bride.

" Now blow thy best, blow thy last,
    My trumpet, for the Right ! " —
He has sent his soul in one strong blast,
    To hearten them that fight.

COMRADES

" Oh, whither, whither, rider toward the west ? "
    " And whither, whither, rider toward the
        east ? "
" I rede we ride upon the same high quest,
    Whereon who enters may not be released :

" To seek the Cup whose form none ever saw, —
    A nobler form than e'er was shapen yet,
Though million million cups without a flaw,
    Afire with gems, on princes' boards' are set ;

" To seek the Wine whereof none ever had
    One draught, though many a generous wine
        flows free, —
The spiritual blood that shall make glad
    The hearts of mighty men that are to be."

" But shall one find it, brother ? Where I ride,
    Men mock and stare, who never had the
        dream.

Yet hope within my breast has never died."
  "Nor ever died in mine that trembling
    gleam."

"Eastward, I deem: the sun and all good
    things
Are born to bless us of the Orient old.'"
"Westward, I deem: an untried ocean sings
  Against that coast, 'New shores await the
    bold.' "

"God speed or thee or me, so coming men
  But have the Cup!" "God speed!" — Not
    once before
Their eyes had met, nor ever met again,
  Yet were they loving comrades evermore.

THE HOUSE OF HATE

MINE enemy builded well, with the soft blue
    hills in sight ;
But betwixt his house and the hills I builded a
    house for spite :
And the name thereof I set in the stone-work
    over the gate,
With a carving of bats and apes ; and I called
    it the House of Hate.

And the front was alive with masks of malice
    and of despair ;
Horned demons that leered in stone, and
    women with serpent hair ;
That whenever his glance would rest on the
    soft hills far and blue,
It must fall on mine evil work, and my hatred
    should pierce him through.

And I said, " I will dwell herein, for beholding
    my heart's desire

On my foe ; " and I knelt, and fain had bright-
  ened the hearth with fire ;
But the brands they would hiss and die, as
  with curses a strangled man,
And the hearth was cold from the day that the
  House of Hate began.

And I called at the open door, " Make ye
  merry, all friends of mine,
In the hall of my House of Hate, where is
  plentiful store and wine.
We will drink unhealth together unto him I
  have foiled and fooled ! "
And they stared and they passed me by ; but
  I scorned to be thereby schooled.

And I ordered my board for feast; and I drank,
  in the topmost seat,
Choice grape from a curious cup ; and the first
  it was wonder-sweet ;
But the second was bitter indeed, and the third
  was bitter and black,
And the gloom of the grave came on me, and
  I cast the cup to wrack.

Alone, I was stark alone, and the shadows
    were each a fear;
And thinly I laughed, but once, for the echoes
    were strange to hear;
And the wind in the hallways howled as a
    green-eyed wolf might cry,
And I heard my heart: I must look on the
    face of a man, or die!

So I crept to my mirrored face, and I looked,
    and I saw it grown
(By the light in my shaking hand) to the like
    of the masks of stone;
And with horror I shrieked aloud as I flung my
    torch and fled,
And a fire-snake writhed where it fell; and at
    midnight the sky was red.

And at morn, when the House of Hate was a
    ruin, despoiled of flame,
I fell at mine enemy's feet, and besought him
    to slay my shame;
But he looked in mine eyes and smiled, and
    his eyes were calm and great:
"You rave, or have dreamed," he said; "I
    saw not your House of Hate."

THE ARROWMAKER

DAY in, day out, or sun or rain,
Or sallow leaf, or summer grain,
Beneath a wintry morning moon
Or through red smouldering afternoon,
With simple joy, with careful pride,
He plies the craft he long has plied :
To shape the stave, to set the sting,
To fit the shaft with irised wing ;
And farers by may hear him sing,
    For still his door is wide :
  "Laugh and sigh, live and die, —
    The world swings round ; I know not, I,
    If north or south mine arrows fly ! "

And sometimes, while he works, he dreams,
And on his soul a vision gleams :
Some storied field fought long ago,
Where arrows fell as thick as snow.

His breath comes fast, his eyes grow bright,
To think upon that ancient fight.
Oh, leaping from the strainèd string
Against an armored Wrong to ring,
Brave the songs that arrows sing!
    He weighs the finished flight:
  "Live and die; by and by
    The sun kills dark; I know not, I,
    In what good fight mine arrows fly!'

Or at the gray hour, weary grown,
When curfew o'er the wold is blown,
He sees, as in a magic glass,
Some lost and lonely mountain-pass;
And lo! a sign of deathful rout
The mocking vine has wound about, —
An earth-fixed arrow by a spring,
All greenly mossed, a mouldered thing;
That stifled shaft no more shall sing!
    He shakes his head in doubt.
  "Laugh and sigh, live and die, —
    The hand is blind: I know not, I,
    In what lost pass mine arrows lie!
    One to east, one to west,

Another for the eagle's breast, —
The archer and the wind know best ! "
The stars are in the sky ;
He lays his arrows by.

A NEST IN A LYRE

As sign before a playhouse serves
    A giant Lyre, ornately gilded,
On whose convenient coignes and curves
    The pert brown sparrows late have builded.
They flit, and flirt, and prune their wings,
    Not awed at all by golden glitter,
And make among the silent strings
    Their satisfied ephemeral twitter.

Ah, somewhat so we perch and flit,
    And spy some crumb and dash to win it,
And with a witty chirping twit
    Our sheltering Time — there 's nothing in it !
In Life's large frame, a glorious Lyre's,
    We nest, content, our season flighty,
Nor guess we brush the powerful wires
    Might witch the stars with music mighty.

THISBE

THE garden within was shaded,
   And guarded about from sight ;
The fragrance flowed to the south wind,
   The fountain leaped to the light.

And the street without was narrow,
   And dusty, and hot, and mean ;
But the bush that bore white roses,
   She leaned to the fence between :

And softly she sought a crevice
   In that barrier blank and tall,
And shyly she thrust out through it
   Her loveliest bud of all.

And tender to touch, and gracious,
   And pure as the moon's pure shine,
The full rose paled and was perfect, —
   For whose eyes, for whose lips, but mine !

THE Puritan Spring Beauties stood freshly
    clad for church ;
A Thrush, white-breasted, o'er them sat sing-
    ing on his perch.
" Happy be ! for fair are ye ! " the gentle singer
    told them,
But presently a buff-coat Bee came booming
    up to scold them.
  "Vanity, oh, vanity !
    Young maids, beware of vanity !"
    Grumbled out the buff-coat Bee,
    Half parson-like, half soldierly.

The sweet-faced maidens trembled, with pretty,
    pinky blushes,
Convinced that it was wicked to listen to the
    Thrushes ;
And when, that shady afternoon, I chanced
    that way to pass,

They hung their little bonnets down and looked
    into the grass.
    All because the buff-coat Bee
    Lectured them so solemnly : —
" Vanity, oh, vanity !
    Young maids, beware of vanity ! "

KINSHIP

A LILY grew in the tangle,
  In a flame-red garment dressed,
And many a ruby spangle
  Besprinkled her tawny breast.

And the silken moth sailed by her
  With a swift and a snow-white sail;
Not a gilt-girt bee came nigh her,
  Nor a fly in his gay green mail.

And the bronze-brown wings and the golden,
  O'er the billowing meadows blown,
Were still as by magic holden
  From the lily that flamed alone;

Till over the fragrant tangle
  A wanderer winging went,
And with many a ruby spangle
  Were his tawny vans besprent.

And he hovered one moment stilly
  O'er the thicket, her mazy bower,
Then he sank to the heart of the lily,
  And they seemed but a single flower.

COMPENSATION

THE brook ran laughing from the shade,
  And in the sunshine danced all day:
The starlight and the moonlight made
  Its glimmering path a Milky Way.

The blue sky burned, with summer fired:
  For parching fields, for pining flowers,
The spirits of the air desired
  The brook's bright life to shed in showers.

It gave its all that thirst to slake;
  Its dusty channel lifeless lay;
Now softest flowers, white-foaming, make
  Its winding bed a Milky Way.

WHEN WILLOWS GREEN

WHEN goldenly the willows green,
  And, mirrored in the sunset pool,
Hang wavering, wild-rose clouds between :
  When robins call in twilights cool:
      What is it we await ?
      Who lingers and is late ?
What strange unrest, what yearning stirs us
      all
When willows green, when robins call ?

When fields of flowering grass respire
  A sweet that seems the breath of Peace,
And liquid-voiced the thrushes choir,
  Oh, whence the sense of glad release ?
      What is it life uplifts ?
      Who entered, bearing gifts ?
What floods from heaven the being overpower
When thrushes choir, when grasses flower ?

AT THE PARTING OF THE WAYS

COMRADE Youth! Sit down with me
Underneath the summer tree,
Cool green dome whose shade is sweet,
Where the sunny roadways meet.
See, the ancient finger-post,
Silver-bleached with rain and shine,
Warns us like a noon-day ghost :
That way 's yours, and this way 's mine!
I would hold you with delays
Here at parting of the ways.

Hold you! I as well might look
To detain the racing brook
With regrets and grievance tender,
As my comrade swift and slender,
Shy, capricious, all of spring !
Catch the wind with blossoms laden,
Catch the wild bird on the wing,
Catch the heart of boy or maiden !

Yet I 'll hold your image fast,
As this hour I saw you last, —
As with staff in hand you sat,
Soft curls putting forth defiant
From the tilted Mercury's hat,
Wreathen with the wilding grace
Of the fresh-leaved vine and pliant,
Stealing down to see your face.
Eyes of pleasance, lips of laughter,
I shall hoard you long hereafter;
Very dear shall be the days
Ere the parting of the ways!

Shall you deem them dear, in truth,
Days when we, o'er hill and hollow,
Trudged together, Comrade Youth?
Ah, you dream of days to follow!
Hand in hand we jogged along;
I would fetch from out my scrip,
Crust or jest or antique song, —
Live and lovely, on your lip.
Such poor needments as I had
Were as yours; you made me glad.
— Lo, the dial! No prayer stays
Time, at parting of the ways!

This gold memory — rings it true?
Half for me and half for you.
Cleave and share it.   Now, good sooth,
God be with you, Comrade Youth !

THE FAIR GRAY LADY

WHEN the charm at last is fled
    From the woodland stark and pale,
And like shades of glad hours dead
    Whirl the leaves before the gale :

When against the western fire
    Darkens many an empty nest,
Like a thwarted heart's desire
    That in prime was hardly guessed :

Then the fair gray Lady leans,
    Lingering, o'er the faded grass,
Still the soul of all the scenes
    Once she graced, a golden lass.

O'er the Year's discrownèd sleep,
    Dear as in her earlier day,
She her bending watch doth keep,
    She the Goldenrod grown gray.

THE ENCOUNTER

THERE 's a wood-way winding high,
Roofed far up with light-green flicker,
Save one midmost star of sky.
Underfoot 't is all pale brown
With the dead leaves matted down
One on other, thick and thicker ;
Soft, but springing to the tread.
There a youth late met a maid
Running lightly, — oh, so fleetly !
" Whence art thou ? " the herd-boy said.
Either side her long hair swayed,
Half a tress and half a braid,
Colored like the soft dead leaf.
As she answered, laughing sweetly,
On she ran, as flies the swallow ;
He could not choose but follow
Though it had been to his grief.

" I have come up from the valley, —
From the valley ! " Once he caught her,

Swerving down a sidelong alley,
For a moment, by the hand.
"Tell me, tell me," he besought her,
" Sweetest, I would understand
Why so cold thy palm, that slips
From me like the shy cold minnow?
The wood is warm, and smells of fern,
And below the meadows burn.
Hard to catch and hard to win, oh !
Why are those brown finger tips
Crinkled as with lines of water ? "

Laughing while she featly footed,
With the herd-boy hasting after,
Sprang she on a trunk uprooted,
Clung she by a roping vine ;
Leaped behind a birch, and told,
Still eluding, through its fine,
Mocking, slender, leafy laughter,
Why her finger tips were cold :

"I went down to tease the brook,
With her fishes, there below ;
She comes dancing, thou must know,
And the bushes arch above her ;

But the seeking sunbeams look,
Dodging, through the wind-blown cover,
Find and kiss her into stars.
Silvery veins entwine and crook
Where a stone her tripping bars;
There be smooth, clear sweeps, and swirls
Bubbling up crisp drops like pearls.
There I lie, along the rocks
Thick with greenest slippery moss,
And I have in hand a strip
Of gray, pliant, dappled bark;
And I comb her liquid locks
Till her tangling currents cross;
And I have delight to hark
To the chiding of her lip,
Taking on the talking stone
With each turn another tone.
Oh, to set her wavelets bickering!
Oh, to hear her laughter simple,
See her fret and flash and dimple!   .
Ha, ha, ha!"   The woodland rang
With the rippling through the flickering.
At the birch the herd-boy sprang.

On a sudden something wound
Vine-like round his throbbing throat;

On a sudden something smote
Sharply on his longing lips,
Stung him as the birch bough whips :
Was it kiss or was it blow ?
Never after could he know ;
She was gone without a sound.

Never after could he see
In the wood or in the mead,
Or in any company
Of the rustic mortal maids,
Her with acorn-colored braids ;
Never came she to his need.
Never more the lad was merry ,
Strayed apart, and learned to dream,
Feeding on the tart wild berry ;
Murmuring words none understood, —
Words with music of the wood,
And with music of the stream.

SUMMER HOURS

Hours aimless-drifting as the milkweed's down
  In seeming, still a seed of joy ye bear
  That steals into the soul when unaware,
And springs up Memory in the stony town.

72

LOVE UNSUNG

Seven jewelled rays has the Sun fast bound
  In his arrow of blinding sheen ;
But he quickens the breast of the fruitful
    ground
  With a subtlest ray unseen.

And the rainbow moods of this love of ours
  I may blend in the song I bring ;
But the magic that makes life laugh with flowers
  Is the love that I cannot sing.

73

THE WISH FOR A CHAPLET

VINELEAF and rose I would my chaplet make :
I would my word were wine for all men's sake,
Pure from the pressing of the stainless feet
Of unblamed Hours, and for an altar meet.

Vineleaf and rose : I would, had I the art,
Distil, to lasting sweet, Joy's rosy heart,
That no sere autumn should its fragrance
      wrong,
Closed in the crystal glass of slender song.

74

SONNETS

THE TORCH-RACE

BRAVE racer, who hast sped the living light
With throat outstretched and every nerve
    a-strain,
Now on thy left hand labors gray-faced Pain,
And Death hangs close behind thee on the
    right.
Soon flag the flying feet, soon fails the sight,
With every pulse the gaunt pursuers gain ;
And all thy splendor of strong life must
    wane
And set into the mystery of night.

Yet fear not, though in falling, blindness hide
Whose hand shall snatch, before it sears the
    sod,
The light thy lessening grasp no more controls :
Truth's rescuer, Truth shall instantly provide :
This is the torch-race game, that noblest souls
Play on through time beneath the eyes of
    God.

TO SLEEP

ALL slumb'rous images that be, combined,
To this white couch and cool shall woo thee,
    Sleep!
First will I think on fields of grasses deep
In gray-green flower, o'er which the transient
    wind
Runs like a smile; and next will call to mind
How glistening poplar-tops, when breezes
    creep
Among their leaves, a tender motion keep,
Stroking the sky, like touch of lovers kind.

Ah, having felt thy calm kiss on mine eyes,
All night inspiring thy divine pure breath,
I shall awake as into godhood born,
And with a fresh, undaunted soul arise,
Clear as the blue convolvulus at morn.
— Dear bedfellow, deals thus thy brother,
    Death?

SISTER SNOW

PRAISED be our Lord (to echo the sweet phrase
Of saintly Francis) for our sister Snow :
Whose soft, soft coming never man may know
By any sound ; whose down-light touch allays
All fevers of worn earth. She clothes the days
In garments without spot, and hence doth go
Her noiseless shuttle swiftly to and fro,
And very pure, and pleasant, are her ways.

But yesterday, how loveless looked the skies !
How cold the sun's last glance, and unbenign,
Across the field forsaken, russet-leaved !
Now pearly peace on all the landscape lies.
—Wast thou not sent us, Sister, for a sign
Of that vast Mercy of God, else unconceived ?

RETROSPECT

"BACKWARD," he said, "dear heart, I like to
    look
To those half-spring, half-winter days, when
    first
We drew together, ere the leaf-buds burst.
Sunbeams were silver yet, keen gusts yet shook
The boughs. Have you remembered that kind
    book,
That for our sake Galeotto's part rehearsed,
(The friend of lovers, — this time blessed, not
    cursed !)
And that best hour, when reading we forsook ?"

She, listening, wore the smile a mother wears
At childish fancies needless to control ;
Yet felt a fine, hid pain with pleasure blend.
Better it seemed to think that love of theirs,
Native as breath, eternal as the soul,
Knew no beginning, could not have an end.

THE CONTRAST

HE loved her ; having felt his love begin
With that first look, — as lover oft avers.
He made pale flowers his pleading ministers,
Impressed sweet music, drew the springtime in
To serve his suit ; but when he could not win,
Forgot her face and those gray eyes of hers ;
And at her name his pulse no longer stirs,
And life goes on as though she had not been.

She never loved him ; but she loved Love so,
So reverenced Love, that all her being shook
At his demand whose entrance she denied.
Her thoughts of him such tender color took
As western skies that keep the afterglow.
The words he spoke were with her till she
    died.

A MYSTERY

THAT sunless day no living shadow swept
Across the hills, fleet shadow chasing light,
Twin of the sailing cloud : but mists wool-
    white,
Slow-stealing mists, on those heaved shoulders
    crept,
And wrought about the strong hills while they
    slept
In witches' wise, and rapt their forms from
    sight.
Dreams were they ; less than dream, the
    noblest height
And farthest ; and the chilly woodland wept.

A sunless day and sad : yet all the while
Within the grave green twilight of the wood,
Inscrutable, immutable, apart,

Hearkening the brook, whose song she under-
    stood,
The secret birch-tree kept her silver smile,
Strange as the peace that gleams at sorrow's
    heart.

TRIUMPH

THIS windy sunlit morning after rain,
The wet bright laurel laughs with beckoning
 gleam
In the blown wood, whence breaks the wild
 white stream
Rushing and flashing, glorying in its gain;
Nor swerves nor parts, but with a swift disdain
O'erleaps the boulders lying in long dream,
Lapped in cold moss; and in its joy doth
 seem
A wood-born creature bursting from a chain.

And "Triumph, triumph, triumph!" is its
 hoarse
Fierce-whispered word. O fond, and dost not
 know
Thy triumph on another wise must be, —
To render all the tribute of thy force,
And lose thy little being in the flow
Of the unvaunting river toward the sea!

IN WINTER, WITH THE BOOK WE READ IN SPRING

The blackberry's bloom, when last we went this
way,
Veiled all her bowsome rods with trembling
white;
The robin's sunset breast gave forth delight
At sunset hour; the wind was warm with May.
Armored in ice the sere stems arch to-day,
Each tiny thorn encased and argent-bright;
Where clung the birds that long have taken
flight,
Dead songless leaves cling fluttering on the
spray.

O hand in mine, that mak'st all paths the same,
Being paths of peace, where falls nor chill nor
gloom,
Made sweet with ardors of an inward spring!

I hold thee — frozen skies to rosy flame
Are turned, and snows to living snows of
    bloom,
And once again the gold-brown thrushes sing.

SERE WISDOM

I HAD remembrance of a summer morn,
When all the glistening field was softly
    stirred
And like a child's in happy sleep I heard
The low and healthful breathing of the corn.
Late when the sumach's red was dulled and
    worn,
And fainter grew the trite and troublous
    word
Of tristful cricket, that replaced the bird,
I sought the slope, and found a waste forlorn.

Against that cold clear west, whence winter
    peers,
All spectral stood the bleachèd stalks thin-
    leaved,
Dry as papyrus kept a thousand years,

And hissing whispered to the wind that
 grieved,
It was a dream — we bare no goodly ears —
There was no summer - time — deceived! de-
 ceived!

ISOLATION

WHITE fog around, soft snow beneath the tread,
All sunless, windless, tranced, the morning
    lay ;
All noiseless, trackless, new, the well-known
    way.
The silence weighed upon the sense : in dread,
" Alone, I am alone," I shuddering said,
" And wander in a region where no ray
Has ever shone, and as on earth's first day
Or last, my kind are not yet born or dead."

Yet not afar, meanwhile, there faltered feet
Like mine, through that wide mystery of the
    snow,
Nor could the old accustomed paths divine ;
And even as mine, unheard spake voices low,
And hearts were near, that as my own heart
    beat,
Warm hands, and faces fashioned like to mine.

THE LOST DRYAD

(TO EDITH M. THOMAS)

INTO what beech or silvern birch, O friend
Suspected ever of a dryad strain,
Hast crept at last, delighting to regain
Thy sylvan house ? Now whither shall I wend,
Or by what wingèd post my greeting send,
Bird, butterfly, or bee ? Shall three moons
    wane,
And yet not found ? — Ah, surely it was pain
Of old, for mortal youth his heart to lend
To any hamadryad ! In his hour
Of simple trust, wild impulse him bereaves :
She flees, she seeks her strait enmossèd bower :
And while he, searching, softly calls, and
    grieves,
Oblivious, high above she laughs in leaves,
Or patters tripping talk to the quick shower.

A MEMORY

Though pent in stony streets, 't is joy to know,
'T is joy, although we breathe a fainter air,
The spirit of those places far and fair
That we have loved, abides ; and fern-scents
    flow
Out of the wood's heart still, and shadows grow
Long on remembered roads as warm days
    wear ;
And still the dark wild water, in its lair,
The narrow chasm, stirs blindly to and fro.

Delight is in the sea-gull's dancing wings,
And sunshine wakes to rose the ruddy hue
Of rocks ; and from her tall wind-slanted stem
A soft bright plume the goldenrod outflings
Along the breeze, above a sea whose blue
Is like the light that kindles through a gem.

THE GIFTS OF THE OAK

(FOR THE SEVENTIETH BIRTHDAY OF JAMES RUSSELL
LOWELL)

'THERE needs no crown to mark the forest's
    king.'
Thus, long ago, thou sang 'st the sound-heart
    tree
Sacred to sovereign Jove, and dear to thee
Since first, a venturous youth with eyes of
    spring, —
Whose pilgrim-staff each side put forth a
    wing, —
Beneath the oak thou lingeredst lovingly
To crave, as largess of his majesty,
Firm-rooted strength, and grace of leaves that
    sing.

He gave; we thank him! Graciousness as
    grave,
And power as easeful as his own he gave;

Long broodings rich with sun, and laughters
     kind ;
And singing leaves, whose later bronze is dear
As the first amber of the budding year, —
Whose voices answer the autumnal wind.

THE STRAYED SINGER

(MATTHEW ARNOLD)

HE wandered from us long, oh, long ago,
Rare singer, with the note unsatisfied;
Into what charmèd wood, what shade star-eyed
With the wind's April darlings, none may
    know.
We lost him. Songless, one with seed to sow,
Keen-smiling toiler, came in place, and plied
His strength in furrowed field till eventide,
And passed to slumber when the sun was low.

But now, — as though Death spoke some
    mystic word
Solving a spell, — present to thought appears
The morn 's estray, not him we saw but late;
And on his lips the strain that once we heard,
And in his hand, cool as with Springtime's
    tears,
The melancholy wood-flowers delicate.

ONE soiled and shamed and foiled in this
world's fight,
Deserter from the host of God, that here
Still darkly struggles, — waked from death in
fear,
And strove to screen his forehead from the
white
And blinding glory of the awful Light,
The revelation and reproach austere.
Then with strong hand outstretched a Shape
drew near,
Bright-browed, majestic, armored like a knight.

"Great Angel, servant of the Highest, why
Stoop'st thou to me?" although his lips were
mute,
His eyes inquired.   The Shining One replied:
"Thy Book, thy birth, life of thy life am I,
Son of thy soul, thy youth's forgotten fruit.
We two go up to judgment side by side."